Guido van Genechten

Well Done, Little White Fish!

Clavis

NEW YORK

Little crab **can cut** sea grass with his claws...

What can Little White Fish do?

Turtle **can carry** a heavy rock on his back.

And what can Little White Fish do?

Sea urchin easily **does** seven **somersaults** in a row.

And Little White Fish? What can he do?

Little jellyfish **can light up** the dark.

No, Little White Fish can't do that!

starfish can stand on one leg
for a very, very long time.

Oops, Little white Fish
doesn't even have legs....

Octopus **can spit out** huge clouds of **ink**.

But what can Little White Fish do?

Sea snake **can make a beautiful arch.**

And Little White Fish?
He swims nimbly over and under it, ten times in a row.

Yes, Little White Fish **can swim really well,**
even backwards and upside down!

"Wow! Well done!" his friends all say.
"We can't do that!"

First published in Belgium and Holland by Clavis Uitgeverij, Hasselt – Amsterdam, 2016
Copyright © 2016, Clavis Uitgeverij
English translation from the Dutch by Clavis Publishing Inc. New York
Copyright © 2017 for the English language edition: Clavis Publishing Inc. New York
Visit us on the web at www.clavisbooks.com

Well Done, Little White Fish! written and illustrated by Guido van Genechten
Original title: Wat knap, klein wit visje!
Translated from the Dutch by Clavis Publishing

ISBN 978-1-60537-327-0

This book was printed in October 2016 at Publikum d.o.o., Slavka Rodica 6, Belgrade, Serbia

First Edition
10 9 8 7 6 5 4 3 2 1